THIS BLOOMSBURY BOOK

BELONGS TO

....

For my parents, Mary and Paul

BLOOMSBURY
CHILDREN'S
BOOKS

First published in Great Britain in 1998 by Bloomsbury Publishing Plc
38 Soho Square, London W1V 5DF
This paperback edition first published 1999

Illustrations copyright © Matilda Harrison 1998
The moral right of both the author and illustrator has been asserted

A CIP catalogue record of this book is available from the British Library
ISBN 0 7475 4124 8 PB
ISBN 0 7475 3556 6 HB
Printed and bound in Belgium by Proost NV, Turnhout

1 3 5 7 9 10 8 6 4 2

Bisky Bats and Pussy Cats

THE ANIMAL NONSENSE OF EDWARD LEAR

Matilda Harrison

BLOOMSBURY
CHILDREN'S
BOOKS

Limericks

There was a Young Lady whose Bonnet,
Came untied when the birds sat upon it
But she said, 'I don't Care!
All the birds in the Air
Are welcome to sit on my Bonnet.'

There was an Old Man on whose Nose,
Most birds of the air could repose;
But they all flew Away,
At the closing of Day,
Which relieved that Old Man and his Nose.

There was a Young Lady of Ryde,
Whose Shoe-strings were seldom untied;
She purchased some Clogs,
and some small spotty Dogs,
And frequently walked about Ryde.

The Pelican Chorus

King and Queen of the Pelicans we;
No other Birds so grand we see!
None but we have feet like fins!
With lovely leathery throats and chins!

Ploffskin, Pluffskin, Pelican jee!
We think no Birds so happy as we!
Plumpskin, Ploshkin, Pelican jill!
We think so then, and we thought so still!

We live on the Nile. The Nile we love.
By night we sleep on the cliffs above.
By day we fish, and at eve we stand
On long bare islands of yellow sand.
And when the sun sinks slowly down
And the great rock walls grow dark and brown,

Where the purple river rolls fast and dim
And the Ivory Ibis starlike skim,
Wing to wing we dance around, –
Stamping our feet with a flumpy sound, –
Opening our mouths as Pelicans ought,
And this is the song we nightly snort:

Ploffskin, Pluffskin, Pelican jee!
We think no Birds as happy as we!
Plumpskin, Ploshkin, Pelican jill!
We think so then, and we thought so still!

Last year came out our Daughter, Dell;
And all the Birds received her well.
To do her honour, a feast we made
For every Bird that can swim or wade.
Herons and Gulls, and Cormorants black,
Cranes, and Flamingoes with scarlet back,
Plovers and Storks, and Geese in clouds,
Swans and Dilberry Ducks in crowds.
Thousands of Birds in wondrous flight!
They ate and drank and danced all night,
And echoing back from the rocks you heard
Multitude-echoes from Bird and Bird, –

Ploffskin, Pluffskin, Pelican jee!
We think no Birds as happy as we!
Plumpskin, Ploshkin, Pelican jill!
We think so then, and we thought so still!

Yes, they came; and among the rest,
The King of the Cranes all grandly dressed.
Such a lovely tail! Its feathers float
Between the ends of his blue dress-coat;
With pea-green trousers all so neat,
And a delicate frill to hide his feet, –
(For though no one speaks of it, everyone knows,
He has got no webs between his toes!)

As soon as he saw our Daughter Dell,
In violent love that Crane King fell, –
On seeing her waddling form so fair,
With a wreath of shrimps in her short
white hair,
And before the end of the next long day,
Our Dell had given her heart away;

For the King of the Cranes had won that heart,
With a Crocodile's egg and a large fish-tart.
She vowed to marry the King of the Cranes,
Leaving the Nile for stranger plains;
And away they flew in a gathering crowd
Of endless Birds in a lengthening cloud.

Ploffskin, Pluffskin, Pelican jee!
We think no Birds as happy as we!
Plumpskin, Ploshkin, Pelican jill!
We think so then, and we thought so still!

And far away in the twilight sky,
We heard them singing a lessening cry, –
Farther and farther till out of sight,
And we stood alone in the silent night!
Often since in the nights of June,
We sit on the sand and watch the moon; –

She has gone to the great Gromboolian plain,
And we probably never shall meet again!
Oft, in the long still nights of June,
We sit on the rocks and watch the moon; –
– She dwells by the streams of the Chankly Bore,
And we probably never shall see her more.

Ploffskin, Pluffskin, Pelican jee!
We think no Birds as happy as we!
Plumpskin, Ploshkin, Pelican jill!
We think so then, and we thought so still!

More Limericks

There was an Old Man who said, 'How
Shall I flee from this horrible cow?
I will sit on this stile,
And continue to smile,
Which may soften the heart of that cow.'

There was an Old Person in Gray,
Whose feelings were tinged with dismay;
She purchased two Parrots,
and fed them with Carrots,
Which pleased that Old Person in Gray.

There was an Old Man of Blackheath,
Whose head was adorned by a wreath,
Of lobsters and spice,
Pickled onions and mice,
That uncommon Old Man of Blackheath.

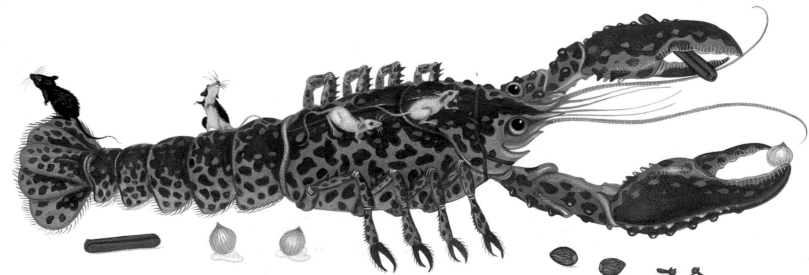

There was a Young Lady of Welling,
Whose praise all the world was telling;
She played on the Harp,
And caught several Carp,
That accomplished Young Lady of Welling.

There was a Young Lady of Bute
Who played on a silver-gilt flute;
She played several jigs,
To her Uncle's pigs,
That amusing Young Lady of Bute.

There was an Old Person of Basing,
Whose presence of mind was amazing;
He purchased a steed,
Which he rode at full speed,
And escaped from the people of Basing.

The Owl and the Pussy-Cat

The Owl and the Pussy-Cat went to sea
In a beautiful pea-green boat,
They took some honey, and plenty of money,
Wrapped up in a five-pound note.
The Owl looked up to the stars above,
And sang to a small guitar,

'O lovely Pussy! O Pussy, my love!
What a beautiful Pussy you are,
You are,
You are!
What a beautiful Pussy you are!'

Pussy said to the Owl, 'You elegant fowl!
How charmingly sweet you sing!
O let us be married! Too long we have tarried;
But what shall we do for a ring?'
They sailed away for a year and a day,
To the land where the Bong-tree grows
And there in a wood a Piggy-wig stood
With a ring at the end of his nose,
His nose,
His nose,
With a ring at the end of his nose.

'Dear Pig, are you willing to sell for one shilling
Your ring?' Said the Piggy, 'I will.'
So they took it away, and were married next day
By the Turkey who lives on the hill.
They dined on mince, and slices of quince,
Which they ate with a runcible spoon;
And hand in hand, on the edge of the sand,
They danced by the light of the moon,
The moon,
The moon,
They danced by the light of the moon.

Even More Limericks

There was a Young Lady of Greenwich,
Whose garments were border'd with spinach,
But a large spotty calf,
Bit her shawl quite in half,
Which alarmed that Young Lady of Greenwich.

There was an Old Person of Ealing,
Who was wholly devoid of good feeling;
He drove a small gig,
With three Owls and a Pig,
Which distressed all the people of Ealing.

There was an Old Man with a beard,
Who said, 'It is just as I feared! –
Two Owls and a Hen,
Four Larks and a Wren,
Have all built their nests in my beard!'

There was an Old Person of Bree,
Who frequented the depths of the sea;
She nursed the small fishes,
And washed all the dishes,
And swam back again into Bree.

There was an Old Person of Bray,
Who sang through the whole of the day;
To his ducks and his pigs,
Whom he fed upon figs,
That valuable person of Bray.

There was an Old Man of Dumbree,
Who taught little owls to drink tea;
For he said, 'To eat mice,
is not proper or nice,'
That amiable man of Dumbree.

The Quangle Wangle's Hat

On the top of the Crumpetty Tree
The Quangle Wangle sat,
But his face you could not see,
On account of his Beaver Hat.
For his Hat was a hundred and two
          feet wide,
With ribbons and bibbons on every side
And bells, and buttons, and loops,
          and lace,
So that nobody ever could see the face
Of the Quangle Wangle Quee.

The Quangle Wangle said
To himself on the Crumpetty Tree, –
'Jam; and jelly; and bread;
Are the best food for me!
But the longer I live on this
          Crumpetty Tree
The plainer than ever it seems to me
That very few people come this way
And that life on the whole is far
          from gay!'
Said the Quangle Wangle Quee.

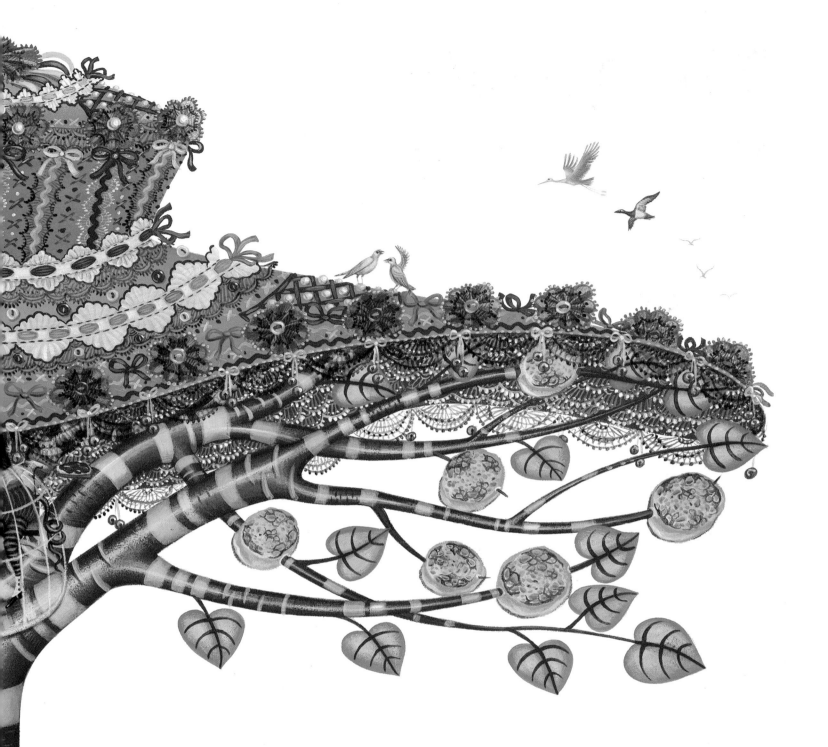

But there came to the Crumpetty Tree,
Mr and Mrs Canary;
And they said, – 'Did you ever see
Any spot so charmingly airy?
May we build a nest on your
      lovely Hat?
O please let us come and build a nest
Of whatever material suits you best,
Mr Quangle Wangle Quee!'

And besides to the Crumpetty Tree
Came the Stork, the Duck, and the Owl;
The Snail, and the Bumble-Bee,
The Frog, and the Fimble Fowl;
(The Fimble Fowl, with a Corkscrew leg;)
And all of them said, – 'We humbly beg,
We may build our homes on your
      lovely Hat, –
Mr Quangle Wangle, grant us that!
Mr Quangle Wangle Quee!'

And the Golden Grouse came there,
And the Pobble who has no toes, –
And the small Olympian bear, –
And the Dong with a luminous nose.

And the Blue Baboon, who played the Flute, –
And the Orient Calf from the Land of Tute, –
And the Attery Squash, and the Bisky Bat, –
All came and built on the lovely Hat
Of the Quangle Wangle Quee.

And the Quangle Wangle said
To himself on the Crumpetty Tree, –
'When all these creatures move
What a wonderful noise there'll be!'

And at night by the light of the Mulberry moon
They danced to the Flute of the Blue Baboon,
On the broad green leaves of the Crumpetty Tree,
And all were as happy as happy could be,
With the Quangle Wangle Quee.

Animal Alphabet

O

The Obsequious Ornamental Ostrich,
who wore Boots to keep his
feet quite dry.

K

The Kicking Kangaroo,
who wore a Pale Pink Muslin Dress
with Blue Spots.

F

The Fizzgiggious Fish,
Who always walked about upon Stilts,
Because he had no legs.

E

The Enthusiastic Elephant,
Who ferried himself across the water with the
Kitchen Poker and a New pair of Ear-rings.

More and More Limericks

There was an Old Man of Dunrose,
A parrot seized hold of his nose;
    When he grew melancholy,
    They said, 'His name's Polly,'
Which soothed that Old Man of Dunrose.

There was an Old Man in a Tree,
Whose whiskers were lovely to see;
    But the Birds of the Air,
    Pluck'd them perfectly bare,
To make themselves Nests in that Tree.

There was an Old Person of Skye,
Who waltzed with a bluebottle fly;
    They buzzed a sweet tune,
    To the light of the Moon,
And entranced all the people of Skye.

There was an Old Person in Black,
A Grasshopper jumped on his back;
When it chirped in his ear,
He was smitten with fear,
That helpless Old Person in Black.

There was an Old Man of Marseilles,
Whose daughters wore bottle-green veils;
They caught several fish,
which they put in a dish,
And sent to their Pa at Marseilles.

There was an Old Man of Bulak,
Who sat on a crocodile's back;
But they said, 'Tow'rds the night,
He may probably bite,'
Which might vex you, Old Man of Bulak.